American Frontier #4

DAVY CROCKETT
AT THE ALAMO
Based on the Walt Disney Television Show

Written by Justine Korman
Cover Illustrated by Mike Wepplo
Illustrated by Charlie Shaw

DISNEY PRESS
NEW YORK

FIRST EDITION
1   3   5   7   9   10   8   6   4   2

Library of Congress Catalog Card Number: 91-71350
ISBN 1-56282-009-5/1-56282-008-7 (lib. bdg.)

Consultant: Judith A. Brundin, Supervisory Education Specialist
National Museum of the American Indian
Smithsonian Institution, New York

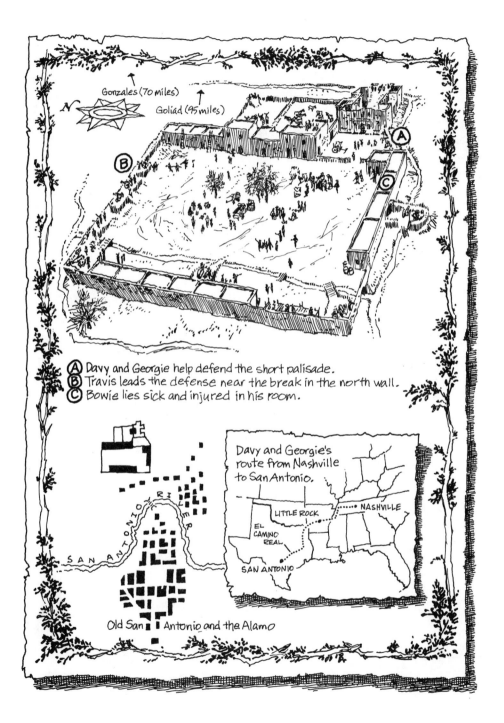

N

Gonzales (70 miles)
Goliad (95 miles)

A Davy and Georgie help defend the short palisade.
B Travis leads the defense near the break in the north wall.
C Bowie lies sick and injured in his room.

SAN ANTONIO RIVER

Davy and Georgie's
route from Nashville
to San Antonio.

LITTLE ROCK — NASHVILLE
EL CAMINO REAL
SAN ANTONIO

Old San Antonio and the Alamo

CHAPTER 1

"Reckon we're just in time," Davy Crockett said when he spotted the riverboat *Delta Queen* rocking gently at the dock. It was New Year's Eve 1835 and Davy and his best friend Georgie Russel had been paddling in a canoe all day to reach the riverboat and join its passengers for the journey down the Mississippi River to Arkansas.

Georgie nodded and they paddled the canoe to shore. Davy bought tickets and he and Georgie boarded the grand steamboat along with elegant-looking passengers in silk gowns and fancy tailcoats. Davy removed his coonskin cap, but even so he and Georgie weren't dressed like the rest of the passengers. They weren't traveling on the *Delta Queen* to ring in the New Year: they were going to Texas to fight for the rights of all Americans.

Later that evening Davy and Georgie had dinner in the *Delta Queen*'s brass and velvet dining hall. Over the noise of the chugging engine and the sound of forks on china, they heard a man call out in a singsong voice.

"Prestidigitation, Ladies and Gentlemen. An old and honorable art. No trickery is involved. See for yourselves. Neither voodoo nor hoodoo. Just watch the little pea."

The man sat beneath a hanging oil lamp. He wore a brown velvet coat trimmed with lace cuffs and a red silk handkerchief at his neck. He beckoned the passengers to come closer.

"Step right up, folks!" he called to the gathering crowd. "Don't be shy. Let the amazing Tiberius Thimblerig dazzle you!"

Done with their meal, Davy and Georgie strolled through the room to see what the fuss was about.

They watched as Thimblerig shuffled three gold thimbles on a table, talking all the while.

"Now you see it, now you don't. Who will try his luck? Who can find the pea? Which thimble is it under?" he asked.

A man with thick white side-whiskers and a bright green vest put up some money and pointed to the thimble on his right. Thimblerig picked it up. There was the pea!

"Well, a man wins, a man loses," Thimblerig said, and he paid the winner. "Fickle fortune, Ladies and

Gentlemen. The hand is not always quicker than the eye."

Just then Thimblerig spotted Davy and Georgie.

"You there in the buckskins," he called. "You look like sharp lads. Here's your chance at edification and profit."

"Edifi-who?" Georgie asked.

"That's just a fancy word for learnin'," Davy said. Then he added to Thimblerig, "I don't hold much for gambling."

"A woodsman and far traveler such as you, afraid of a little game?" Thimblerig taunted.

"I just reckon gamblin' is foolish," Davy replied.

Thimblerig laughed. "Come, now. Is it foolish to win handsomely, as my sharp-eyed friend here did just now?" he asked, pointing to the man in the green vest.

"I'll never gamble to win money," Davy declared. "But let's try this. If I lose, I'll buy refreshments for all these fine folks. If you lose, it's your treat."

"Fair enough," Thimblerig agreed.

Davy watched intently as Thimblerig jumbled the thimbles on the tabletop. Then the gambler stopped.

"Choose!" he cried.

Davy pointed to a thimble.

"So it's there, is it?" Thimblerig asked. "Let's see."

But before he could lift the thimble, Davy grabbed the gambler's wrist.

"I always like to do my own peeking," said Davy. Then he lifted all the thimbles. There wasn't a pea under any one of them! An angry murmur spread through the crowd. Davy pulled Thimblerig's fingers open. There, in the palm of his hand, was the pea.

"Why, you . . . you backwoods—" Thimblerig sputtered, reaching into his gold silk vest. He pulled out a small, pearl-handled pistol.

Georgie chuckled. "Reckon you didn't get my friend's name. Meet Davy Crockett."

"Davy Crockett!" the gambler gasped. Thimblerig may not have recognized Davy, but he sure had heard of him. Truth is, most folks had heard stories about Davy and how strong and brave he was. Everyone knew that Davy had wrestled bears, that he had ended battles between settlers and Indians, and that he had even gotten to be friends with tough old Mike Fink, the undisputed King of the River. Davy was such a legend and so well respected that he had even served three terms in Congress.

Thimblerig quickly lowered his pistol.

Davy grinned. "There's nothin' I like better than a good loser."

Thimblerig shrugged and forced a smile. Knowing there was no way out, he cried, "Fickle fortune strikes me again! Gather 'round one and all! The refreshments are on me!"

While the noisy crowd ate and drank at Thimblerig's expense, Davy and Georgie went out on the deck. They leaned against the riverboat's rail and watched the moonlight ripple on the Mississippi.

"We're almost to Arkansas," said Georgie.

"Yup," said Davy. "We'll still have a ways to go to get to Texas, but they need men to help them real bad. Look at this newspaper article, Georgie."

Georgie stepped under a lantern and read the headline. "Texas Independence Threatened. Mexican General Santa Anna Vows to Expel Settlers."

Texas was a large area of land that belonged to Mexico. Because there was a lot of empty, undeveloped space in Texas, the Mexican government invited American families to settle there. This way, pioneer families got land to live on and farm while the Mexican government got Texas to grow and prosper.

The settlers learned Spanish and got along well with their Mexican neighbors. The land was fertile and the people were happy. Then Santa Anna became president of Mexico. He was a cruel dictator who made life hard for American Texans, and they rebelled.

Santa Anna sent an army to fight the Texans at a fort called the Alamo. The Texans captured the fort and Santa Anna vowed revenge.

Georgie threw the newspaper on the deck and whistled. "Texas!" he said. "What a mess of trouble."

"Americans in trouble," Davy added. "Trouble I aim to fix."

"And I aim to help you," said Georgie. "But in the meantime, I got just one thing to say."

"What's that?" asked Davy.

Georgie grinned. "Happy New Year!"

CHAPTER 2

few days later, Davy and Georgie strolled down the *Delta Queen*'s gangplank. Suddenly Thimblerig came tumbling off the boat and landed on a bale of cotton stacked on the dock. His hat and carpetbag were tossed down after him.

"And don't come back!" shouted the steamboat's sturdy first mate.

"Well I never!" Thimblerig said. He scrambled to his feet, brushing the dust off his clothes.

Georgie threw back his head and laughed. After Davy had exposed him as a cheat, Thimblerig had been kicked off the riverboat. He looked awfully foolish as he tried to collect himself.

Thimblerig shot Georgie a look.

"I fail to see what is so amusing," he said, grasping the wide lapels of his jacket. "I believe I have you gentlemen to thank for this embarrassing change in my travel plans.

"Since you are responsible for stranding me in this savage terrain, perhaps you will consent to let me join you on your journey."

"You mean you want to come along with us?" Georgie asked.

"I am, in point of fact, offering you and Mr. Crockett my incomparable companionship," Thimblerig said with a bow.

"He wants to be friends," Davy explained to Georgie. Davy smiled and turned back to Thimblerig. "Georgie and I figured on heading down Texas way."

"That's fine. Anywhere would be better than here. When do we start?" Thimblerig asked.

Davy looked concerned. "You may not know what you're getting into, Thimblerig."

"Well, what is this Texas? Is it a town? Do they enjoy sophisticated company? Are there . . . any lawmen?" Thimblerig asked. But before Davy could answer, he gushed on. "For delicate reasons I care not to explain . . . I would rather avoid the company of officers of the law."

"You mean the law is after you?" Georgie asked.

Thimblerig blustered, "They're after the wrong man, I assure you. But I'd rather not have to convince them of that. Surely, sir, you will not deny me the pleasure of your illustrious company?"

Davy looked into Thimblerig's eyes. The old trickster was scared. He was a long way from anywhere or anything he knew. He belonged in a big city or on a flashy riverboat. Davy could see that underneath it all, the little man was lost and alone. It'd be downright cruel to leave him out here on his own.

"Well, you're welcome to come with us," Davy said. "If that's all right with you, Georgie?"

"Aw, Davy!" Georgie groaned. "You're always taking in strays."

Davy used the last of his money to buy horses and supplies in a nearby town, and then he, Georgie, and Thimblerig saddled up and rode off into the territory that separated Arkansas from Texas.

Davy was glad to be riding through open country. He'd felt cooped up and out of place on that elegant riverboat.

Thimblerig was very jittery while they traveled through Indian territory, but the three men rode for several days without incident. At last, they splashed across the muddy Red River, which marked the border between the Indian territory and Texas.

Davy cried, "Well, there she is! Texas! All the room a man could hope for."

Davy, Georgie, and Thimblerig rode along a trail called El Camino Real in Spanish, or "the Royal Road." Despite its fancy name, it was just a dusty trail through the wilderness.

The raw wind howled across the treeless plains of tall prairie grass.

"A desolate, dessicated place!" Thimblerig grumbled.

"Better than a jail cell," Georgie pointed out.

Thimblerig turned up his collar and hunched inside his fancy coat.

They stopped to fill their canteens at the first clear stream they saw. Giant pecan trees grew along the bank, and they stuffed their saddlebags with nuts.

"This is good grazing land. A man could raise some mighty fine livestock here," Davy declared. "The air is dry and healthy. And there's room to stretch."

"In other words it's as empty as a poor man's pocket," Georgie groused.

They remounted their horses and rode down a rocky ravine.

"Whoa," Davy said and reined his horse.

The others stopped beside him. Davy cupped one hand to his ear and listened. Georgie cocked his head.

"What's that sound?" Georgie wondered. "Sounds like hoofbeats. A lot of them!"

The ground shook and the cliffs were filled with a rumbling roar.

"What unearthly manifestation is that?" Thimblerig asked. The noise grew even louder.

"Sounds like the whole Comanche nation," Georgie said.

"Comanches!" Thimblerig shrieked.

"I don't know what it is," said Davy. "But I aim to find out."

Davy, Georgie, and Thimblerig left their horses and climbed a ridge. They looked out and saw a buffalo stampede. The beasts' huge hooves pounded the hard, dry dirt, and dust rose in thick clouds.

"There must be thousands of them," Thimblerig said. He stared in awe at the big shaggy beasts. Their huge humped shoulders bobbed like waves on a brown ocean. The sun gleamed on their short, curved horns.

"We were born too late to see buffalo in Tennessee," Georgie said. They had been hunted down to nothing east of the Mississippi.

"Actually, these here are bison," said Davy.

A Comanche whoop suddenly split the air. Thimblerig covered his head with his arms.

"Reckon that's what caused the stampede," said Georgie. He pointed at a lone young man riding his pinto pony into the herd. The hunter waved a lance and whooped again, and a group of buffalo broke from the main herd.

"He's Comanche, all right," said Davy. "And he's headed for trouble. He's aimed straight at a prairie-dog town."

Thimblerig squinted. "I don't see a town. And I don't see any dogs."

"Don't you know anything?" Georgie said.

Davy explained. "Prairie dogs are little critters like chipmunks. They live in burrows underground. A whole mess of them live together, and it's called a town." Davy pointed. "See all those holes? Each one leads into the town. If the Indian's horse steps in a hole—well, you'll see."

Just as Davy said it, the Indian hunter's pony stepped right into a prairie-dog hole. He whinnied and fell. The Comanche was flipped to the hard ground and lay still.

"Yow! That hurt!" Georgie exclaimed.

Davy clambered down the ridge. He carefully felt the hunter's arms and legs to check for broken bones.

After a few moments, the hunter came to. But when he opened his eyes and saw Davy, he pulled out a knife. Davy and the young Comanche hunter wrestled and rolled over the dusty ground. Davy tried to get the knife out of the man's hand, but despite his injuries, the hunter was very strong.

"Need any help, Davy?" Georgie asked, ready to step in.

"Nay," gasped Davy. "He's powerful strong, but he's hurt bad. He'll realize it any second—I hope."

Just then, as if on cue, the Comanche man fainted.

CHAPTER 3

avy carried the hunter to a sheltered spot. He tended to the Comanche's wounds while Thimblerig watched Georgie "hobble" the horses. Georgie tied a short piece of rope between the front and back legs of each horse so they couldn't wander off during the night. Then Georgie and Thimblerig set up camp. The sun was setting and it was getting cold.

"We need a fire," Thimblerig said, and he shivered. He looked around the treeless plain. "What will we do for wood?"

"We don't need wood," Davy said. He grabbed Ol' Betsy, his rifle. "I'll be back directly with dinner. Georgie'll explain about the fire." Davy walked out into the tall grass.

"Thimblerig, my friend," Georgie said. "I have an important job for you. I want you to go out there and gather as many buffalo chips as you can find. There oughtta be plenty."

"Buffalo chips?" Thimblerig asked.

"Yup," said Georgie. "They're round and brown, about yea big." Georgie made a circle with his hands. "Only get the dry ones. You'll know 'em when you see 'em."

Soon Thimblerig returned with an armful of buffalo chips. Georgie took them and stacked them. Then he struck flint and steel together to make a spark. The dried chips quickly caught fire.

Thimblerig stretched out his hands and sighed as the warmth reached his chilled fingers.

"What are these things anyway?" Thimblerig asked.

"Buffalo dung," Georgie said.

Thimblerig's eyes widened for a moment. Then he cleared his throat. "Bison dung," he corrected.

Davy returned with wild prairie birds for dinner. Soon the smell of roasting meat filled the air.

"I can hardly wait to taste that bird," Thimblerig said. He tucked a silk handkerchief under his chin.

The Comanche hunter moaned suddenly, held his bandaged head, and sat up.

"Your friend's awake," Georgie remarked.

"Think I'll have a talk with him," said Davy. He took a plate of food to the Indian man.

Davy spoke no Comanche and the hunter spoke no English, so the two spoke in sign language, using their hands to form words.

"Can Davy actually understand this hand waving?" Thimblerig asked.

"Sure," said Georgie. "He learned it from the Shawnees. Different Indian tribes speak different languages, so they made up a sign language that enabled them to talk to each other and to settlers, too."

"Do you understand sign language?" asked Thimblerig.

"I know some," said Georgie.

"What's he saying now?" Thimblerig asked.

"He says he's a Honey Eater," Georgie said. "That's a friendly tribe of the Comanche. Near as I can make out this feller's had a hard time. The medicine man was upset because he was not good at performing rituals. And on top of that, his pony fell down and he lost the buffalo.

"He says he's by himself," Georgie added. "He says he'd make a good guide, if we need one." He saw Davy nod his head.

"Hey, Davy!" Georgie called. "With all his busted luck, you sure we want him for a guide?"

"He says he's willing to lead us to a water hole one moon to the southwest," Davy said. "Sounds good to me."

"I, for one, do not trust that savage," Thimblerig said haughtily. "How do you know he's really going to take us where he says? He might lead us into a trap."

"Not everyone's a cheater," Davy said.

"Far as I'm concerned," said Georgie, "we've got more reason to trust him than you."

"Nobody knows a trail better than an Indian," Davy said. "And he's our friend now. Besides, he's the only one who knows the way to the next water hole."

Busted Luck, as they called their new guide, was as good as his word. The next day he led them through flat plains and scrubby hills to a water hole. Along the way, he showed them where to gather persimmons, wild plums, and Indian potatoes.

At the water hole, Davy saw two men in ponchos and sombreros resting in the shade of a single stubby tree. One was frail and white haired. The other was middle aged and had the sturdy frame of a farmer.

Beside them sat a woman in a black shawl. She held a baby in her arms. A young girl in a white blouse and embroidered skirt sat nearby.

Not far from the family, a burro sipped from the water hole. His heavy load of household goods lay on the ground.

Davy, Thimblerig, Georgie, and Busted Luck stopped their horses. They climbed down and nodded and smiled to the family.

While his friends filled their canteens, Davy laid Ol' Betsy down and showed his empty hands to the family. Then he walked over to them.

The younger man's right arm was in a sling under

his brown, striped poncho. He used his left hand to doff his gray sombrero.

"Buenos dias," he said.

"Good morning," Davy replied, lifting his coonskin cap.

"Good morning," the man repeated in English. "I am Miguel Rodriguez y Fuentes." He introduced his father, his wife, their daughter, and their infant son.

"I'm Davy Crockett," Davy replied. "Do you know where the settlement of Texas is?"

Miguel looked nervous. "If you mean San Antonio de Bexar," he said, "do not go there!"

"Yup. That's where we're headed," Davy said.

Miguel shook his head. "Generalissimo Santa Anna and his troops are marching closer every day. That is a dangerous place to be, Señor Crockett!"

"Already there has been much fighting," the grandfather said. "In December, Santa Anna's army burned our farm. We were lucky to escape with our lives."

Davy glanced at Miguel's sling.

"I am taking my family to safety," Miguel explained. "We are farmers, not fighters."

"No one wants this Santa Anna. He is a cruel and greedy man. We cannot pay his taxes. All we want is to live in peace," the grandfather said.

"Many people want to fight Santa Anna," said Miguel. "They say Texas should be free. The Tejanos, the rebels, captured the Alamo after a big battle with Santa

Anna's men. But the Generalissimo has an army of thousands! The Tejanos cannot hope to stand against so many."

"Well, we reckoned on helping to even up the odds," Davy said. "We want to join the Tejanos."

"You are brave men. If I did not have a family to protect, I would be fighting, too!" Miguel declared.

Miguel's wife searched through a basket for something. She pulled out a cloth-wrapped package and pressed it into Davy's hands.

"Take this with you for the hungry days ahead," she said. "And may God be with you."

"Thank you, ma'am," Davy said. "Much obliged." Then he turned back to Miguel and asked, "Now whereabouts are these settlers?"

"The Tejanos are barricaded in the Alamo, an old mission across the San Antonio River," the farmer replied.

"It is on El Camino Real. If you follow the road, you will come to San Antonio de Bexar. Cross the town, and you will find the Alamo just beyond," said Miguel.

"You would be wise to reconsider," the grandfather warned.

Davy climbed back on his horse.

" 'Preciate the warning," he said. "But I'm probably as stubborn as that burro of yours, and my mind's made up."

Georgie shouted, "Company forward!"

And they rode away.

Davy and the others spent the entire day riding across the flat, grassy prairie. Cool winter winds fanned the horses' manes and ruffled the fringe on Davy's buckskins. All four men were tired and bored by the unchanging landscape.

Davy told all the stories he could think of to pass the time. Even so, he grew tired of talking. Then Georgie took over, singing trail songs.

But then Georgie ran out of songs. Thimblerig remained quiet, lost in his own thoughts. And Busted Luck had only spoken in sign language so far. Rocked by their horses' steady plodding, the men were almost asleep in the saddle.

Davy's ears perked up at the muffled sound of approaching hoofbeats. He stopped his horse to listen.

"What is it, Davy? More buffalo?" Georgie asked. He and the others reined their horses, too.

Davy looked around. Over a nearby ridge he spotted a group of men on horseback.

"That might be trouble," Davy said.

He squinted at the glare of sunlight bouncing off shiny metal breastplates and glittering lances. "Looks like one of Santa Anna's advance patrols," Davy observed.

In the distance they could hear orders being shouted. They saw the horses on the ridge leap forward into a run—toward them!

The four men galloped off in a hurry. Thimblerig's heart pounded in his chest as the soldiers charged.

"We're doomed!" he shrieked. He hunched low in his saddle as shots whizzed overhead.

"Aw, I've had worse from an angry porcupine," Davy said. But he and the others spurred their horses to go faster.

The enemy soldiers fired wildly. Their horses thundered as they jumped gullies and flattened yucca plants. Flocks of frightened prairie birds fluttered out of the tall grass.

At each shot Thimblerig flinched, praying his horse wouldn't stumble. Busted Luck wasn't afraid. He was used to things going wrong.

CHAPTER 4

Racing across the plains, Thimblerig braved a look over his shoulder. The enemy soldiers were falling behind. He could barely hear the pop of their rifles over the rushing wind, and no more bullets whizzed past his ears.

Thimblerig hoped he and the others had put enough distance between themselves and the cavalry. But suddenly more rifles crackled nearby. Davy reined his horse and veered off in a new direction.

Thimblerig looked up and saw another troop of Santa Anna's men thundering toward them from the opposite direction. He raced after Davy, Georgie, and Busted Luck into the tumbled rocks of a low hill. Davy and Georgie quickly dismounted, crouched behind boulders, and began loading their rifles. Busted Luck joined them and placed an arrow in his bow.

Thimblerig dashed behind them for safety. Davy raised his rifle, took aim, and squeezed the trigger.

An enemy soldier toppled from his saddle and fell to the dusty ground.

"That's one!" Georgie cried. He took aim and fired. Another soldier fell.

But the soldiers were outside the range of Busted Luck's bow, and Davy and Georgie couldn't load and fire nearly fast enough to stop the entire brigade.

"We're doomed!" Thimblerig moaned.

Davy was never the kind to give up, but things did look pretty bad. Several dozen soldiers were bearing down on them with lances and rifles, and there was nothing to do but fight it out.

Suddenly a volley of shots split the air. The enemy suddenly scattered and galloped away as fast as their horses could carry them.

"Weeeee-haaaaaah!" came a holler through the hills.

"It must be Comanche warriors!" Thimblerig said, in a panic.

Georgie chuckled. "Not hardly."

Davy was already standing and waving.

Their rescuers were a party of ten men dressed in fringed buckskins like Davy's and Georgie's. All of them cradled long rifles in their hands.

A big, red-bearded man hopped off his horse and reached out a meaty hand to Davy.

"George MacGregor of the Tennessee Mounted Volunteers," the man said in a booming voice.

"Reckon we're mighty glad you folks stopped by,"

Davy said, shaking MacGregor's hand. He nodded to the other Volunteers.

"Seemed like the neighborly thing to do," MacGregor said.

"I'm Davy Crockett and these here are my friends Georgie Russel, Tiberius Thimblerig, and Busted Luck," Davy announced.

The Volunteers cheered. "Davy Crockett! *The* Davy Crockett?"

"None other," Georgie said.

"What're you doing here?" MacGregor wanted to know. "Not enough bears left in Tennessee?"

Davy laughed. "I'm not on a bear hunt. I heard there was a fight down Alamo way."

"That's where we're headed," MacGregor replied. "I'd be honored if you'd lead our company, Colonel Crockett."

Davy was flattered, but all he wanted was to ride along with the other Volunteers.

The journey to San Antonio de Bexar took two weeks, but the time passed quickly. Even though Thimblerig continued to jump at every sound, they did not encounter any more enemy patrols.

On February 8th, the company of Volunteers topped the hills overlooking San Antonio. Thimblerig sat stiffly in the saddle. He was so sore that he dreamed of burning his saddle and never riding a horse again.

The company rode wearily downslope to the one-

hundred-year-old town on the bank of the winding San
Antonio River.

Busted Luck made a series of hand signals. Davy
laughed.

"What's so funny?" Georgie demanded. He was not
as quick at sign language as Davy.

"Busted Luck was telling me that the Indian name
for this river means 'Drunken-old-man-going-home-at-
night.' "

Georgie and the other men looked at the winding
river and joined in the laughter.

San Antonio was a pretty little town built of white-
washed adobe bricks. The mud bricks were baked hard
in the hot sun and made for thick walls and cool houses.
There were also a few log houses like the one Davy had
left behind in Tennessee.

The tallest building was a church near the center. A
red, white, and green Mexican flag flew from its steeple.

Most of the houses were empty, although the streets
were busy with the few remaining people. They were
hastily preparing to leave before another battle began.
Women in bright dresses balanced baskets of food on
their heads. Donkeys brayed under heavy loads. A family heaped furniture onto a cart.

Scarring the walls of many of the houses were count-
less bullet holes, terrible reminders of the battle that had
taken place there not long before, in December.

Georgie gave a low whistle. "No wonder everyone's clearing out."

On a hill opposite the town sat a walled complex almost as big as the town itself.

"That's the Alamo," MacGregor said.

The Alamo was a large rectangular fort with twelve-foot-high mud-brick walls. In some places the walls were six feet thick. In other places they were even thicker. A deep ditch ran in a line just outside the walls.

The Alamo was first built as a mission, or home, for priests, but they eventually abandoned the site. The Alamo stood empty until the Mexican army converted it into a fort to defend the early settlers in San Antonio against hostile Indian tribes. But, after Santa Anna took over, the Mexican soldiers no longer defended the settlers. They were fighting them.

In December, Colonel Ben Milam and his Texas Volunteers had stormed San Antonio in order to gain independence from Mexico.

During the battle, the Volunteers dug through the thick clay of the Alamo's north wall. Thanks to Milam's clever strategy, the small force defeated the Mexican army!

The Texans allowed the Mexican soldiers to lay down their weapons and go home. Only two Texans, including Ben Milam, were killed.

As the Volunteers got closer, they could make out the

remains of a stone church. What had been the roof of the church was now a heap of rubble.

Davy's horse reared and whinnied. There was a rumble of hooves to the south. A bugle blared. War cries and gunfire shattered the still air. Another patrol of enemy soldiers clattered across the plains.

"Don't look now, but we've got company again," Davy said.

"Sure would be a shame to get shot before we even got to fight," Georgie said.

Thimblerig forgot his saddle sores in a new surge of fear.

Davy and the Volunteers galloped for the safety behind the arched gate of the Alamo. The sharpshooters on the walls drove back the enemy patrol.

The Volunteers reined their horses once they were inside the fort. Sentries closed the big oak gates. Behind the huge walls, the men felt safe. They could hear their enemies sounding retreat on a bugle.

The Tennessee Mounted Volunteers waved to the cheering men on the scorched walls. Some of the Texans wore short blue army jackets over their homespun trousers, but most were dressed in buckskins or farm clothes.

Before the dust had settled around their horses' hooves, the Volunteers were met by a tall, thin man. He wore a neat blue uniform and a wide white hat. His jacket was trimmed with an officer's gold braid. His trousers were carefully pressed into sharp creases. A heavy sword hung from a red sash at his waist.

"That was a tight squeeze. Are you men all right?" the man asked. He had a South Carolina accent.

"I reckon. You in command?" Davy asked.

"I am in charge of the regular army. Colonel William Bennett Travis," the man said. Then he shook Davy's hand.

Davy suspected Travis hadn't seen very much fighting. But you don't judge a tree by its bark, Davy thought. The man might be a fine soldier and a nice feller once you got to know him.

"Colonel Bowie is in command of the Volunteers," Travis added.

"The feller who invented the knife?" Davy wondered. Fighting Jim Bowie was a living legend. No knife was big enough for him so he made his own—it had a foot-long blade that weighed a whole pound.

"The same," Travis said, with a slight frown. "I take it you are an admirer."

"I sure am," Davy said. From the tone of Travis's remark, Davy reckoned he and Bowie might not be the best of friends. It was hard to picture this fussy man getting along with a rough-and-tumble scrapper like Jim Bowie.

"Since he's in charge of the Volunteers, I expect I should go shake hands with him," Davy said.

"Colonel Bowie is in our hospital. He took a fall helping us mount a cannon. A fever's been giving him the devil ever since," Travis explained.

Davy followed the young officer across the plaza of the Alamo. On the right, Davy saw the thick stone walls of the ruined and roofless church. Off to his left, a mighty, big cannon sat on a platform in the southwest corner. Its log ramp crossed over a ditch that ran the length of the compound.

Davy could see that the ditch ran under the walls to connect with the ditch outside. There were a couple of small bridges over the ditch at different places.

Men climbed ladders that leaned against log platforms. Low buildings lined the inside of the east and west walls.

At the far end of the fort, to the north, Davy saw men working to repair a hole in the wall while others nearby worked to construct more gun platforms.

The Alamo still showed the scars of the December battle in its cracked and crumbling plaster and brick. Men carried baskets of dirt and mixed mud and straw to make more adobe bricks.

"There is a lot of work to do," Travis told Crockett.

"And not a lot of time to do it," Davy said.

"We have plenty of time," Travis said calmly. He seemed very sure of himself. "We don't expect Santa Anna to arrive before mid-March. That gives us a good few weeks to prepare."

Davy remembered Miguel's family at the water hole. They'd seemed certain that Santa Anna was already close. And he'd seen enough advance troops to think the main force of the army might not be far behind.

"I heard he was already on his way," Davy said.

"Rumors!" Travis snorted. "I don't believe them."

Davy wondered how Travis could ignore what was right under his nose. He had to have seen the enemy scouts that had nearly kept the Volunteers from reaching the Alamo. But Davy didn't say anything. He reckoned Travis had his reasons.

They reached a scarred two-story building. It had a flat roof and stairs on the outside.

"This is the Long Barracks," Travis said. "Bowie is upstairs."

They climbed the stairs to the second floor. Inside the cool adobe room, a powerfully built man lay on a cot. His face was flushed and sweaty with fever.

Travis saluted. "Colonel Bowie, we have some rein-forcements." Then he added to Davy, "I'll see that your men and horses are taken care of." Travis turned crisply on his heels and marched out of the room.

"Colonel Bowie, I just brought a company in and figured I ought to report," Davy began. "I'm Davy Crockett from Tennessee."

Bowie's face relaxed into an easy smile. He reached up to shake Davy's hand. "Davy Crockett! By the Great

Eternal, I never hoped to see you in this neck of the woods."

"Well, why not?" Davy asked. "Half of Tennessee is here with you and Sam Houston."

Davy remembered Houston as a fearsome fighter in the Red Stick War, when they'd both served under General Andrew Jackson. Houston was a good man who had since made quite a name for himself.

"My old fighting buddies sure have come up in the world," said Davy. "Jackson is president of the United States, and Houston is a general and commander in chief of the Texan army."

"That's because he has the only complete uniform in Texas," Bowie joked, but his laugh quickly changed to a cough. When he caught his breath he apologized, "Can't seem to shake this cough. Tell me, how many men did you bring?"

"Fourteen," Davy said. "Including me."

"Fourteen?" Bowie groaned. "It would take a thousand troops to man this garrison, and I've got less than two hundred Volunteers."

"Two hundred stubborn men can do a tolerable lot of fighting," Davy said.

Bowie looked Davy in the eyes and said, "Maybe I better tell you what our situation here really is. Back in December, I brought a scouting party down here to tell Travis to withdraw. I had orders from Sam Houston to take the men to safety. Got here just after the big battle. Ben Milam and his boys had captured this fort. But after Ben was killed in the battle, Colonel Fannin took charge.

"In all the excitement of winning this fort, Colonel Fannin took some fool notion in his head to invade Mexico. I got here too late to stop him. Fannin took four hundred men and almost all the supplies and wagons. Most of the horses and almost all the ammunition are gone. Last I heard they were all stuck in the town of Goliad, and we're stuck here."

"Colonel Travis doesn't seem worried," Davy pointed out.

Bowie laughed weakly. "If it's not in a book, he doesn't believe it. He's never been in a battle in his life. Travis thinks a good general would wait for the spring grass before he marches his army across the plains," Bowie said. "Now that would make some sense—grass to feed the horses and cattle. But this Santa Anna cares more about revenge than about sensible battle plans. I think he's around the corner, pawing and snorting like an angry bull.

"Some reliable scouts say he's only one hundred fifty miles away. If we can't hold this miserable fort until Houston raises a decent-sized army, Texas is lost!"

"We'll just have to hold her then," Davy said.

"We're practically surrounded already. They've cut off our main water supply. All we've got is a well that's half dry, about enough rations for a fair-sized family dinner back home, and enough powder for a turkey shoot," Bowie said. He looked hard at Davy. "This last part is just between you and me."

"Aren't there any more Texans around?" Davy wondered.

"So far none of our messengers has returned," Bowie said sadly.

"Got a fresh horse? I'll take a crack at it," Davy volunteered.

Bowie shook his head. "No, Davy. We need your breed of man here. We both know the amount of powder in the gun's not nearly as important as the spirit of the man holding the rifle.

"Crockett, for the first time since I've been here I believe we can hold out," Bowie said. He sat up with renewed strength.

Davy held up his rifle and took Bowie's big knife in his other hand.

"Between Ol' Betsy here and your Arkansas toothpick, how can we lose?" Davy asked.

CHAPTER 5

Over the next two weeks, everyone worked hard to repair the old mission and turn it back into a sturdy fort. Davy got to know most of the men as they worked side by side.

The men hailed from every corner of the United States and Mexico. The youngest was William Malone, an eighteen year old from Georgia, who was away from home for the first time. Robert Moore, a fifty-five year old from Virginia, was the oldest member of the garrison. There was little Henry Warnell, a horse-racing jockey from Arkansas, and Davy Cummings from Pennsylvania, who had come just to deliver a box of rifles to Sam Houston but had decided to stay. Many in the ranks were Mexican civilians who had also settled in Texas and suffered under Santa Anna.

Green Jameson was the Alamo's chief engineer. He was in charge of rebuilding and strengthening the fort.

Green continually paced the thick walls and studied the situation. The December battle had caused a great deal of damage. Green assigned men to fill in the hole in the north wall where the Texan rebels had dug their way in when they captured the fort. There was also a gap in the south wall between the low barracks and the ruined church that needed fixing.

Almeron Dickerson was a young blacksmith who commanded the Alamo's cannon batteries. The Mexicans had left more than twenty cannons in the fort when they were driven out. Dickerson had gotten eighteen in good working order. But the big guns were useless without gun platforms. Without platforms, the cannons could not shoot over the high walls. Green and Dickerson discussed how and where to build the platforms.

Sam Blair, in charge of ammunition, was worried. The supply of ammunition was running very low because Colonel Fannin had taken most of it with him.

The men didn't have many cannonballs, so Blair organized a crew to chop up horseshoes. The chunks of metal could be stuffed into a cannon and fired just like a ball.

"Puts me in mind of when my daddy could only spare me one bullet a day," Davy said while he helped. "I practiced till I could shoot the wick off a candle at three hundred paces! With only one bullet, I couldn't afford to miss."

* * *

Later that day, Davy joined the Volunteers who were patching weak spots in the wall. When they'd finished that, Green set them to work on the south wall to fill the gap between the ruined church and the low barracks.

"This palisade will protect the south gate," Green told the sweating men.

"What's a palisade?" asked Lafe. The young Tennessee Volunteer leaned on the handle of his shovel. He wiped his brow with a bright red handkerchief.

"*Palisade* is just a fancy word for a wall," Georgie told him. He wiped his sweaty face with his sleeve. "Hard as it is to say, it's sure harder to make!"

"How nice to know there's a term for this form of torture," Thimblerig complained. His blistered hands were wrapped in rags.

Davy didn't mind splitting logs. He'd built his own cabins, and worked hard all his life. But there never was a job that didn't go down easier with a good story. And Davy sure enjoyed telling some pretty tall tales. In fact, his stories were part of what made him such a legend.

"Wish I'd brought my pet bear, Death Hug," Davy said. "He can lift a tolerable lot of logs when he wants to. But mostly he prefers reading—whenever he can find his glasses."

The men chuckled, but Davy was just warming up.

"Now Death Hug is a mighty fine bear, but I really need my wildcat. Back home he does all my chores."

"What can he do?" Lafe asked.

Davy grinned. "He tends my garden, puts wood on the fire, and when I get cold at night he does my shivering for me."

The men were having such a good time listening to Davy they hardly noticed that they'd finished the palisade. They had erected two log walls only three feet apart and filled the space between them with dirt.

Next, Green ordered the men to put up gun platforms inside the north and west walls. As they worked, Davy told them all about his pet alligator, Old Mississippi. The big old alligator would give him a ride home from hunting if Davy got tired.

As the day wore on toward evening, though, the talk turned serious.

"I don't think the messengers to Goliad ever made it," MacGregor said. "We've heard nary a word from Colonel Fannin."

"Fannin'll be here with guns blazing!" Lafe insisted. "Colonel Travis says so."

"One of the regulars showed me a map. Goliad's way down by the Gulf of Mexico," MacGregor replied grimly. "It's nearly a hundred miles from here."

"Well that's just a hop, skip, and a jump," Davy said. "We came fifteen hundred miles from Tennessee."

"Yeah, but it's awfully close to the Mexican border," said another man, Louis Rose.

"One of our scouts saw a long convoy of Santa Anna's troops nearing the Rio Hondo," Robert Moore said, changing the subject slightly. "He must be whipping them boys something fierce to keep them marching in this cold weather."

"The Rio Hondo's only fifty miles from here," Rose said.

"They can't be crossing the river or the plains now," Lafe said. "The water's freezing, and there's no grass for the animals once they reach the other side."

"I heard the scout reporting to Travis with my own ears," Moore said.

"I don't doubt your word," Davy said, "but let's not get our britches in a knot before we know for sure."

Rose snorted. "Travis hasn't said a word to any of us. What do you think he's hiding?"

Travis's stern voice startled them. He was standing on the wall above.

"I suggest you tend to your duty, soldier. You have better things to do than talk a lot of nonsense."

But that very night the advance guard of the invading army set up camp on the Rio Hondo.

Santa Anna planned to attack immediately, but a sudden rainstorm raised the river and the raid was called off. Although a seasoned soldier and ruthless leader, Santa Anna had a terrible fear of water. Crossing the Rio Hondo filled him with dread.

*　　*　　*

The next day, young William Malone was posted as a lookout high up in the belfry of the San Antonio church. He blinked in the bright sun as flashes of light, like hundreds of mirrors, winked on the prairie.

Malone rubbed his eyes. The lights rose over a low ridge, and when he looked closer, he could just make out horses and riders holding shiny lances. Malone stared down at the awesome sight of Santa Anna's huge army.

He yanked the thick ropes to ring the church's bell. Santa Anna was here!

Malone scrambled down the belfry stairs. He burst through the church doors into the dusty streets of San Antonio. He was breathless by the time he reached the walls of the fortress.

The heavy gates swung open and Malone was quickly surrounded by men eager to know why he had rung the bell.

Davy's firm hand steadied Malone's heaving shoulders.

"Santa Anna!" the boy gasped.

Travis stared for a moment, confused.

"He's here," Malone said, still panting.

"To the southwest," reported the sentry on the gate.

Travis and Davy ran up the slope of a platform. They squinted into the distance. They saw thousands of dark dots glinting with steel and gold.

Davy saw Travis's face fall. Suddenly the calm and composed young colonel looked badly frightened. But Travis quickly pulled himself together.

Captain Juan Seguin volunteered to ride to Gonzales to ask for more reinforcements. Even though Travis was still certain men were already on their way back from Goliad, he agreed to let Seguin go. It was clear now that they would need all the help they could get.

As the brave captain rode off, Travis assembled a special squad. Davy and Georgie were among the men chosen to leave the fort to forage for supplies. They didn't have much time, and they knew this would be their last chance to stock up.

They saddled up their horses and trotted out the main gate. On the walls above, eagle-eyed sharpshooters stood ready to protect them.

It was too dangerous to go into San Antonio. Santa Anna's scouts had already entered the town. But there was a cluster of farmhouses near the Alamo's southwestern corner. The people had left their homes in such a hurry that there was bound to be some food left.

The men fanned out swiftly to search the houses, fields, and barns. Whoever had lived in the house Davy searched had left most of their furniture. The glass doors of an empty china cabinet yawned open. A bouquet of dead flowers remained in the center of the dining table. A few toys were scattered on the dirt floor.

In the kitchen, Davy found some moldy cheese and

stale tortillas. He was glad to get outside again. To Davy, the house felt haunted by the memory of lives torn apart by war.

Out in the barn, Davy found sacks of dried corn. Lafe had also gotten lucky. He had found a whole side of bacon hanging in a smokehouse. All Georgie had found was a bag of half-rotten potatoes.

Then MacGregor shouted, "We have to go back!" He pointed to San Antonio down the hill. Beyond the winding river, Davy could see a column of soldiers snaking through the streets. Bright flags fluttered above their plumed hats and shining bayonets. There was a rattle of drums and the faint blare of bugles.

The squad quickly loaded their horses with the scraps of food they had found. It wasn't much, but every bit would help. A couple of men led cattle they had found in the fields.

They heard more bugle calls and spurred their horses to go faster. The squad was safely inside the Alamo when the enemy overran the farmhouses.

Dusk settled over the Texas plains. Up on the wall, Georgie surveyed Santa Anna's swarming legions. There were already too many to count, and more arrived every hour.

"Look at that camp out there. There's twice as many as there were last night. I bet there's two thousand of them by now. Bad as ants at a picnic."

"Now, Georgie, the more targets a man has to shoot at, the easier they are to hit," Davy replied.

"They'll make it easy with those fancy, bright uniforms," Georgie scoffed. But his heart sank seeing the hordes of soldiers riding into San Antonio.

"What're they doing over by the church?" Davy wondered. He watched a group of soldiers remove the red, white, and green flag of Mexico from the steeple, and raise another flag in its place. A blood red banner was unfurled. It twisted and writhed in the wind like a crimson serpent.

A chill ran through the mission. Every man knew what the red flag meant: No mercy!

CHAPTER 6

Davy looked around at the men. He knew they were thinking about how outnumbered they were by Santa Anna's troops. It was unlikely that the Mexican army would be ready to attack that night, but when they did. . . .

Davy firmly believed that brooding never did anyone any good, so he decided to take matters into his own hands with the help of a fiddle.

"Hey, this ain't no funeral!" Davy hollered. "MacGregor, get your bagpipes! Let's have us a hoe-down!"

The men gathered around as Davy and MacGregor staged a musical duel to see who could play the loudest and the longest. The rest of the men stopped thinking about their worries and began to shout encouragement to the musicians.

Davy smiled over his fiddle. This is what we're

fighting for, he thought. The right to be free and happy.

After a few songs, MacGregor stopped to catch his breath, and Davy put fresh rosin on his bow. Before they could start the next tune, Colonel Travis came up and tapped Davy on the shoulder.

"Sorry to interrupt, Crockett, but Colonel Bowie wants to see you." Davy handed the fiddle to Georgie, and he and Travis hurried to Bowie's quarters by the south gate.

"How is he?" Davy asked.

"Not well, I'm afraid," Travis answered, as he and Davy entered Bowie's room.

"Boys, I have to do something I've never done before," Bowie said wearily. "I'm quitting. I owe it to the men. I'm in no shape for command. One of you has to take over for me."

"The men elected *you*, Colonel. They don't find much to look up to in me, I'm afraid," Travis said.

It was true. Most of the men saw him as too stiff and removed, and they also had their doubts about his experience. Travis had never been in a battle before, and although he usually did his best not to show it, he had some doubts of his own.

He turned to Davy. "I'd be proud to take orders from Colonel Crockett. All the men look up to him."

"Why, tarnation, man," said Davy. "Round such

military men as you and Jim Bowie I don't reckon I'm much more than a high private."

"But you're the most famous fighting man of our time," Travis argued.

"In Tennessee, maybe, but Texas is your country," Davy said. "I only came to give you Texans a helping hand."

"He's right, Travis," Bowie said. "You and I share command. You're the logical choice to take over."

Travis bit his lip and frowned. There would be no getting out of this.

"All right, sir," Travis finally agreed. "I know I can count on you for help, though, Colonel Crockett."

"Just put me and the Tennessee boys where you want us. We'll do whatever you want done," Davy promised.

"Well, how would you like to take over the south wall?" Travis suggested. "That's our weakest point."

"That'll suit us just fine," Davy said.

Bowie nodded, then sighed heavily. "There's something else. Word's getting around that things are looking pretty grim for us."

Davy nodded. "That's as true as preachin'."

"You'll recall that Ben Milam, rest his soul, let the Mexican army soldiers go home when we captured the Alamo," Bowie began. "I'm hoping I can get the same terms from Santa Anna. I feel responsible for bringing many of the men here. Sam Houston wanted us to pull out, but Fannin took all the wagons on his fool mission. So here we are.

"I can't say I'm too hopeful about what Santa Anna will say," Bowie admitted. "But it's worth a shot."

"No harm in trying," Davy agreed.

A few hours later, after night had fallen, a courier returned with Santa Anna's reply to Bowie's request. He handed Travis a sealed scroll, and Travis quickly untied the ribbon, unrolled a long piece of paper, and read its contents.

"There's a lot of fancy script that, roughly translated, means 'surrender or die,' " he told Davy angrily.

"Well, I'm not much of an authority on surrendering," Davy said.

"Neither am I!" Travis declared. "Cannon master! Santa Anna is waiting for our answer. Let's give it to him—all eighteen pounds!"

Dickerson loaded the big cannon.

"Fire in the hole!" Travis ordered.

Dickerson fired the cannon, and with a loud boom, a heavy iron ball went hurtling into enemy lines.

The rest of the night was quiet. There was no response to Travis's cannonball, but at daybreak, the men of the Alamo saw a grim sight. Santa Anna's gunners had dug trenches on the riverbanks. Row upon row of shining brass cannons now crouched by the water, their muzzles pointed at the Alamo.

Davy and Georgie saw the cannons flash and smoke before they heard the first explosions.

Davy ducked as a heavy ball hit the wall not ten feet from where he was standing. The blast nearly rocked him off his feet and sprayed plaster and fragments of brick across the plaza. As Davy shook the dust from his coonskin cap, another ball struck the western gun platform. Davy watched the now-splintered logs collapse beneath the weight of the cannon.

Dickerson screamed orders while a gun crew hurried to load the mighty eighteen-pounder in the southwest corner of the fort.

The battle had begun!

Perched on the log palisade between Davy and Georgie, the exhausted Thimblerig bemoaned his fate. He was hungry and dirty, and his nerves were jangled from the last four days and nights of constant shelling.

"They say that war is the most exciting experience a man can endure. For me it's the most miserable method of suicide," he complained.

The air was thick with the stench of gunpowder and with the rumble and roar of bomb bursts.

"Shelled us four nights and shelled us four days, but they haven't hit a man yet," Davy observed.

"Yet," Thimblerig emphasized.

Georgie snickered. "Don't worry, Thimblerig, you're too shifty to hit!"

Just then, the shelling stopped. The men's ears rang with the sudden silence.

Travis called to Davy and his men from the ground. "Better get some food and rest while you can."

"I'll get us some feed," Georgie told Davy, and he scrambled down from the wall as Travis climbed up to talk to Davy.

"Some of the boys are worn pretty thin," Davy told Travis. No one had slept during the shelling or had eaten much in the last four days.

Travis nodded. "I know," he said. "But four days and no casualties," he went on. "I wonder how long our luck will hold."

"Luck? This is the hand of providence," Davy said. "We'll win this one yet." He looked at the Alamo flag waving over the battered walls.

Travis marveled at Davy's confidence and easy manner. Despite the lack of food and sleep, and the endless explosions, Davy seemed as comfortable as if he were chatting by his fireside back home.

"You really believe that?" Travis asked.

Davy nodded. "Sure do."

Travis smiled, his courage renewed.

"So do I, Mr. Crockett. So do I."

CHAPTER 7

"*Viva Santa Anna!*" cheered a squad of enemy soldiers as they stormed the Alamo's south wall two days later.

Davy leveled Ol' Betsy at a crimson-coated invader. After six days of siege—a chance to fight at last!

The defenders ran to the south wall. They shot as fast as they could load, aiming their rifles carefully, trying to make each bullet count. There was little ammunition to spare.

The men fired until their rifles were too hot to touch. Many enemy soldiers fell in the dusty fields below before the red-coated troops finally retreated through clouds of gunsmoke.

While the defenders were busy beating back the attack at the south wall, the enemy moved their cannons closer to the north wall, where there weren't enough sharpshooters to keep them from advancing. As they got closer to the walls, the cannons were able to do more damage.

While the battle raged, the Texans worked hard to shore up battered walls and to reset guns knocked from their mounts by ferocious blasts.

Whenever there was a pause in the shelling, the defenders took turns standing watch while others ate at their stations.

Thimblerig complained to Captain Dickerson and Busted Luck. "Corn and beef for breakfast. Beef and corn for lunch. And not enough of either. It's difficult to maintain manly courage on these portions."

Thimblerig held out his plate. On the dull metal there were small dabs of cooked corn and tough beef, not much more than a handful of each. It was not a filling meal.

"It's better than nothing," Dickerson said. "But not much."

"Would you care to tempt Lady Luck, double or nothing?" Thimblerig offered. He took his golden thimbles from his vest pocket.

Dickerson considered the scraps on his plate. "What do you mean?"

"If you guess the position of the pea beneath my thimbles, you may enjoy both my meal and yours," Thimblerig explained. "If, however, you fail to guess correctly, I shall partake of the combined feast."

"You mean, if I win I get your dinner and if you win you get mine?" Dickerson asked.

"Precisely," Thimblerig replied.

Dickerson shrugged. "Why not? My stomach won't miss this."

Thimblerig handed the two plates to Busted Luck. "You hold the stakes, my friend."

Busted Luck watched with interest as Thimblerig arranged the golden thimbles on the top of his dirty gray hat. He knew this game. The Iowa Indians played it with moccasins. He carefully watched Thimblerig.

"Neither voodoo nor hoodoo," Thimblerig chanted, speedily shuffling the thimbles. "Now you see it, now you don't."

Thimblerig's hands stopped. The thimbles stood in a ragged row on his hat. "Choose!"

Dickerson leaned forward and peered at the shiny thimbles. At last he picked the middle one. Thimblerig lifted it, but there was no pea beneath.

Dickerson shrugged and walked away. Thimblerig happily reached for the two plates.

Busted Luck stopped the gambler with a hand signal and pointed to his own plate. Thimblerig had spent enough time with Busted Luck to understand his hand signs. He realized that Busted Luck wanted to play, too.

"Very well," he said. Once again, Thimblerig shuffled the thimbles.

Busted Luck pointed to a thimble, but before Thimblerig could lift it, Busted Luck grabbed his hand, pried open his fingers, and uncovered the pea hidden in his palm.

Thimblerig was too thunderstruck to protest. Busted Luck emptied all the plates onto his own and ate with gusto.

Thimblerig ate the pea—and ended his career as a gambler.

"Who goes there?" a sentry shouted.

Thimblerig snapped awake. He heard galloping horses.

"What now?" he moaned. He had been dreaming of a juicy steak dinner served on gold plates. He was just sinking his teeth into a steaming baked potato when the sentry's call shocked him back to cold, hungry reality.

"Halt!" the sentry repeated, raising his rifle. The hooves clattered to a stop.

"We're on your side," an angry voice shouted in the darkness below.

Thimblerig sighed with relief. An excited murmur was heard among the groggy men. Reinforcements were here at last!

The gates opened wide, and a small company of riders trotted into the Alamo. Travis greeted their commander, a dark-haired man who swung down from his saddle and saluted.

"Captain Martin of the Gonzales Militia," he said. "Captain Juan Seguin sent us before riding on to Goliad. He hopes to get word of what reinforcements are on the way from there.

"We had to creep between the tents of Santa Anna's eastern column to get here. There were a couple of times when we thought we would not make it."

"You see?" Lafe told MacGregor triumphantly. "Help is on the way."

MacGregor just shrugged. He had counted the number of new men.

"Thirty-two more men against thousands."

"Goliath didn't think much of Davy's slingshot, but he found out size doesn't mean everything," said Davy.

"That's tellin' 'em, Davy," Georgie said. "I reckon we could take out a whole regiment of these boys with slingshots, if we had to."

The next day was a lot like the last few. The roar and crash of cannon fire jolted the fort, jarred the men's nerves, and frayed their tempers.

Repair work was constant. Food and water were scarce. The defenders sucked on pebbles to keep their mouths from getting too dry.

Colonel Bowie had his cot carried around the fort, so he could offer words of encouragement to the troops.

Despite his pain, Bowie joked with each man and recalled past adventures. Just seeing the colonel boosted the men's spirits.

When night fell, most of the defenders crawled inside their blankets while Davy continued to watch for enemy patrols. Georgie crept up beside him.

"How are you doing?" he whispered.

"Keeping awake," Davy replied, yawning.

"Say, Davy. I just found out something from one of Martin's men," Georgie said slowly. "He says we're sitting here like a bunch of treed possums. We're just about out of ammunition and there's no more help coming."

Davy nodded. "I've known that since the day we got here, but we're still holding out."

"You've known since then?" Georgie was indignant. Before Davy could explain, he stomped off and went straight to find Colonel Travis. The colonel was asleep in his clothes on a cot, his sword and shotgun resting beside him. He woke with a start and aimed his gun while blinking the sleep from his eyes.

"Mr. Russel?" Travis asked, staring bleary eyed at Georgie. "What do you want?" He sat up and straightened his uniform.

"I want out of here," Georgie said.

"This is no prison. You can go any time you want," Travis said coldly. He thought Georgie was deserting.

"I'm not scared of fighting, but this won't be a fair fight," Georgie said. "We're surrounded by Santa Anna's army, we're nearly out of ammunition, and as far as we know, there's no help on the way."

"Did you wake me to tell me this?" Travis asked impatiently.

"I'm not sure you *are* awake," Georgie said testily. "I came to see you 'cause I'm the man for the job."

Travis was puzzled. "You're not talking about deserting?"

"No, sir. I want to ride to Goliad and stir us up some help," Georgie said. "I know I can make it. I've been in and out of bear traps all my life and I haven't lost any toes yet. I want to go right now."

"Very well," said Travis. "I'll have Colonel Bowie's horse saddled. It's the fastest in the fort." He handed Georgie a well-worn map.

"We'll fire the eighteen-pounder at dawn each day while you're gone, so you'll know we've not surrendered."

That night, at midnight, some of Travis's men hauled sandbags away from the opening of the drainage ditch which ran under the Alamo's walls. Georgie led Bowie's horse through the narrow tunnel and slipped out. Sharpshooters on the north wall distracted the enemy army with gunfire.

Georgie's horse galloped past the high banks of the

drainage ditch and then they were out in the open. Georgie barely saw the scores of tents and enemy soldiers leaping to their feet at the sound of hooves. He only heard the bark of commands and the sound of shots behind him. As his horse raced across the prairie, Georgie thought of Davy's favorite saying, "Just be sure you're right, and then go ahead!"

CHAPTER 8

The eighteen-pound cannon boomed its signal at dawn on Saturday, March 5th. Georgie had been gone for two days.

The Mexican cannons were now only two hundred yards away from the Alamo. They surrounded the fort on all four sides.

"Come closer!" Lafe yelled to the gunners. "You need to have your pretty red coats ventilated!" But the enemy stayed just outside rifle range.

Suddenly a fresh volley of cannonballs came hurtling into the Alamo. Stone chips flew like hail across the plaza and choking dust drifted like fog. The walls were crumbling faster than the weary defenders could shore them up.

Davy rubbed his burning eyes and surveyed the fields outside the walls. Row upon row of red, blue, and white uniforms stretched as far as the eye could see. Santa Anna's armies formed a huge web blanketing the fields and the town. Davy's heart tightened with fear for Georgie. If he did make it back from Goliad, he'd be stuck like a fly in a spider's web.

Some of the enemy soldiers were making ladders with which they planned to climb the Alamo walls. It looked like it wouldn't be long before the enemy rushed the mission.

Davy saw his fellow defenders crouched on the barricade of the south wall. They were all staring at the army filling the fields.

"Reminds me of your herd of buffalo," Davy said to Busted Luck.

"Bison," Thimblerig corrected, wiping his forehead with the tattered, filthy remains of one of his lace cuffs.

Davy chuckled. It was time to stir things up a bit and show some spirit. He clutched Ol' Betsy and cried, "Come closer, you varmints! I'm Davy Crockett, fresh from the backwoods of Tennessee! I'm half horse and half alligator, with a touch o' snappin' turtle. I've got the fastest horse, the prettiest sister, the surest rifle, and the ugliest dog in Tennessee. My father can lick any man in Kentucky, and I can lick my father. I can hug a bear too close for comfort and shoot the tail off a kite in a March wind!"

The Texans cheered and waved their hats. The Tennessee Volunteers whooped, "That's telling 'em, Davy!"

Enemy cannon fire blasted the top of the wall in a return gesture. A Texas gunner wheeled his cannon over to fire back. But Davy said, "Save that big popgun. It eats too much powder. They're close enough to aim our rifles at now, ain't they, Lafe?"

The Tennessee sharpshooter grinned.

"Mighty obliging of them to move in so close, Davy," Lafe said.

"I could use a little target practice myself," Colonel Travis added with a grim smile.

The three men fired their rifles and the enemy gunners fell to the ground.

"That's more like it," said Davy. He rose to his feet to reload. He ignored the shots that went whistling past his coonskin cap.

Thimblerig's stomach growled. He'd been setting aside half of his meager rations since Georgie left. He was determined to leave, too, and figured he would need food for the trip. Now his only problem was finding the courage and the way. He envied Georgie, who for better or for worse was, at least, gone!

Louis Rose kept saying they were all fools to stay. He, himself, was just waiting for the right time to escape, he told Thimblerig.

To Thimblerig, every day seemed like the right day to leave. Each night he dreamed of being free of the scorched walls. The only reason he hadn't left already was that he was even more scared to go than to stay. He shuddered at all the possible dangers. Even if he made it past enemy lines, a wrong turn might put him in hostile Indian territory, or he could starve to death in some wilderness. What he needed was a guide.

All day between the rumbling cannons, Thimblerig had tried to get a moment alone with Davy. He hoped Davy would agree to lead a group out of the Alamo. But Davy was always busy. If he wasn't shoring up a wall or heaving sandbags, he was lifting the men's spirits by singing songs and playing the fiddle, or telling one of his tall tales.

When Thimblerig finally told Davy his plan, Davy stroked his chin thoughtfully, then spoke with quiet reassurance.

"I know things don't look good, but we can win this fight," he said.

Thimblerig sighed and walked away. If Davy wouldn't help, maybe someone else would. He went to find Rose, but the man seemed to have disappeared.

"Maybe he's gone already!" Thimblerig worried. He was getting desperate. He sat on the wall and looked out at the rising smoke of campfires dotting the plains.

As the day faded into night, Thimblerig continued to stare into the distance, pondering his predicament. Suddenly he saw a series of tiny bright sparks, followed by faint pops of gunfire. He could just make out the dust trail of a lone rider dodging a hail of bullets.

Thimblerig stood up and cried, "It's Georgie!"

"Open the gate!" Davy hollered.

Georgie and his horse squeezed through the huge doors even as the defenders pulled them open. One look at Georgie, and Davy knew the news wasn't good.

"Back to your posts," Travis commanded his men, and he turned to Georgie. "How many men will come from Goliad?"

Georgie gave his report. "They can't spare any. They're pinned down by another column of Santa Anna's army. Captain Seguin never made it."

"You came *back* to tell us that!" Davy said. "You idiot! You were safe—why'd you come back?"

"Just got lonesome, I reckon," Georgie joked.

Davy smiled. It was good to have Georgie back. He noticed a slash of blood across Georgie's left cheek.

"They notched you up with their bullets like an old razorback," Davy said.

"Aw, they can't shoot for sour apples," Georgie replied. He hastily wiped the blood off his face.

Travis said, "Crockett, we can't keep this from the men. I'll assemble the troops. You better break it to Colonel Bowie."

While Davy went to tell Bowie the bad news, Thimblerig spoke to Georgie.

"You had every chance to be free and clear," he marveled. "Yet you came back." Then he handed Georgie the pouch of food he had been hoarding for his escape.

"A hero's repast," Thimblerig said. He tucked the shredded remains of his silk handkerchief under Georgie's chin.

Georgie was surprised. "Why that's mighty kind of you," he said. It seemed to him that a meal had never tasted so good.

CHAPTER 9

cross the river in San Antonio, General Antonio
López de Santa Anna and his officers studied the
plans for the next attack. Santa Anna was so sure
of victory that he had already ordered special medals for
his troops.

"There is one thing that concerns me," said Captain
Soldano. He then reported tales of a sharpshooter on the
southern palisade.

"The soldiers fear the tall man in buckskins," Soldano said. "They say he never misses. Some of the men
refuse to go near his station."

"Do not waste my time with this," Santa Anna said.
He pounded his fist on the table. "One man is nothing.
Power is everything."

Santa Anna outlined his plan of attack one more
time. A column of infantry would charge each side of
the Alamo. The cavalry would wait to pick off Texans
if they tried to escape. Couriers had already taken his

orders to the unit commanders. The Alamo would fall!

Jim Bowie tossed on the twisted sheets of his cot. Fever raged through his exhausted body. A soft knock on the door woke him. In the darkened room he could just make out Davy Crockett.

"Mighty good of you to keep looking in on me," he said.

"When a man's laid up, he gets awful tired of his own company," Davy said. "And glad to see a friend's face."

"Friends for such a short time," Bowie said sadly. "It's a shame we didn't meet sooner."

"We'd have had some good hunting trips all right," Davy agreed.

"Tell you what," Bowie said. "When we finish this job we'll go looking for lost silver mines."

Davy nodded.

"It's awful quiet out there," Bowie said.

"Georgie just made it back from Goliad," Davy said. "No help coming."

Bowie was thoughtful, then he said, "I brought those men in here. I reckon I better be with them now. Give me a hand, Davy."

"Take it easy, Colonel," Davy said, "I'll get you outside." He called the two guards by Bowie's room and they hurried in to carry the colonel.

From his perch on the north wall, Colonel Travis looked over the torchlit fort, noting every detail as if he were trying to fix it in his memory. He saw Bowie being carried out beside the well, where the men stood assembled, waiting for Travis's announcement.

Travis sighed, then straightened up and went to address his men. It was a cold, dark night. The moon was hidden behind clouds, and the Mexican guns were silent for the moment.

"I've called you all together because it's time you knew the truth," Travis began in a clear, measured voice. "Russel brings us bad news, men. The defense of the Alamo rests on us alone. There will be no help from Goliad."

The men exchanged worried glances and murmured comments.

Travis held his hands up for order. "Things are bad. Santa Anna has nearly five thousand men massed against us. I cannot force you to stay and fight unless you believe in our cause as strongly as I do. While it's still dark, there is time to slip off to safety. I won't blame any man who does not stay."

Rose had reappeared and stood by Thimblerig's side. "Y'hear?" he hissed. "Time to get out while the getting's good."

Thimblerig wavered. What good could he do here? Why not leave with Rose?

Travis swept out his sword and drew a line in the

dust. "Those who will stay and fight, cross over the line."

"Hornbuckle! Contreras!" Bowie called. His hefty guards lifted his cot, carried the commander over the line, and then stood proudly beside him.

Davy stepped over the line next, with Georgie right behind him, followed by Busted Luck. The rest of the defenders began to move across the line.

Thimblerig hesitated, looking between Rose and Davy. Then he squared his shoulders and stepped over the line.

The defenders smiled at each other and stood proudly together. They knew the battle wouldn't be easy, but they would stick together. They hardly noticed as one man—Rose—slunk off into the night.

Davy knew that liberty was never won easily. It demanded courage and determination, and Davy felt proud to be in such brave company. He and the others would defend the Alamo to the bitter end. They knew they were right, and they would go ahead!

EPILOG

Davy Crockett is perhaps the most famous folk hero of the American frontier. He was born in 1786 and grew up in the rugged country of eastern Tennessee, where his father ran a small country inn. Business was never very good, and the family often relied on young Davy's hunting skills to put food on the table. But even in tough times, Davy had a knack for amusing himself and others with tall tales, a skill that was to later become part of the Crockett legend.

In 1806, Davy married Polly Finley, and they began to raise a family. As the frontier grew more crowded with settlers, Davy and Polly kept moving their family farther west. In 1813, Davy and his family moved for the last time, deep into western Tennessee.

Davy championed the rights of Native Americans in an era marked by great injustice toward Indian people. In 1813, he joined the army in an effort to negotiate an end to the Creek War. His efforts were successful, and in the process he earned the respect of both sides.

Davy returned from the war a hero and was so popular that

he was eventually elected to the United States Congress, where he served three terms. During that time, he helped draft a treaty that would have enabled the Indian people to keep their land. But in 1835, when Congress decided to break the treaty, and his efforts to save it failed, he decided not to run for reelection.

In 1836, Davy Crockett, along with his trusted companion Georgie Russel, joined a small band of brave American settlers under siege at the Alamo in San Antonio, Texas, which was then part of Mexico. The settlers fought long and valiantly in the name of freedom to defend themselves against the Mexican Army, but in the end their numbers were no match for the huge force amassed against them. The enemy soldiers finally overran the Alamo, killing every man, woman, and child within its walls. Davy Crockett died as he had lived—an American hero. And the phrase "Remember the Alamo!" lived on to inspire and unite the Americans in Texas, who eventually won their freedom from Mexico and brought Texas into the United States.